Karen's Campout

Look for these
and other books about Karen
in the
Baby-sitters Little Sister series:

1 Karen's Witch

2 Karen's Roller Skates

3 Karen's Worst Day

4 Karen's Kittycat Club

5 Karen's School Picture

6 Karen's Little Sister

7 Karen's Birthday

8 Karen's Haircut

9 Karen's Sleepover

#10 Karen's Grandmothers

#11 Karen's Prize .

#12 Karen's Ghost

#13 Karen's Surprise

#14 Karen's New Year

#15 Karen's in Love

#16 Karen's Goldfish

#17 Karen's Brothers

#18 Karen's Home Run

#19 Karen's Good-bye

#20 Karen's Carnival

#21 Karen's New Teacher

#22 Karen's Little Witch

#23 Karen's Doll

#24 Karen's School Trip

#25 Karen's Pen Pal

#26 Karen's Ducklings

#27 Karen's Big Joke

#28 Karen's Tea Party

#29 Karen's Cartwheel

#30 Karen's Kittens

#31 Karen's Bully

#32 Karen's Pumpkin Patch

#33 Karen's Secret

#34 Karen's Snow Day

#35 Karen's Doll Hospital

#36 Karen's New Friend

#37 Karen's Tuba

#38 Karen's Big Lie

#39 Karen's Wedding

Super Specials:

1 Karen's Wish

2 Karen's Plane Trip

3 Karen's Mystery

4 Karen, Hannie, and
Nancy: The Three
Musketeers

5 Karen's Baby

6 Karen's Campout

Little Sister

Karen's Campout
Ann M. Martin

Illustrations by Susan Tang

A
LITTLE APPLE
PAPERBACK

SCHOLASTIC INC.
New York Toronto London Auckland Sydney

Activities by Nancy E. Krulik

Activity illustrations by Alfred Giuliani

ISBN 0-590-46911-8

12 11 10 9 8 7 6 5 4 3 2 1   3 4 5 6 7 8/9

Printed in the U.S.A.   40

First Scholastic printing, July 1993

*The author gratefully acknowledges
Stephanie Calmenson
for her help
with this book.*

KAREN

"*Three days! Two days! One day! Fun day!*"

That was my countdown-to-camp song. I was singing it to Goosie, my stuffed cat.

"It is summer vacation," I said. "In three more days I will be going to Camp Mohawk."

Hi. I am Karen Brewer. I am seven years old. I have blonde hair, blue eyes, and some freckles. When I am at Camp Mohawk, I will get more freckles from being in the sun. I will probably get a pink nose, too. That

1

will not be too bad. My pink nose will go with my pink glasses. They are the glasses I wear most of the time, except when I am reading. When I am reading, I wear my blue glasses.

"Goosie, I am sorry you cannot come to camp with me. You are still too little for sleep-away camp. So is Andrew," I explained.

Andrew is my brother. He is four-going-on-five.

Do you want to know who else is *not* going to camp with me? I will tell you: Mommy, Seth (my stepfather), Emily Junior (my pet rat), Rocky (Seth's cat), and Midgie (Seth's dog). They all live at the little house in Stoneybrook, Connecticut. That is where I live most of the time.

Here are the rest of the people and pets who are *not* going to camp with me: Daddy, Elizabeth (my stepmother), Kristy (my step-sister, who is thirteen, and the best step-sister in the whole world), Sam and Charlie (my big stepbrothers, who are in high school), Emily Michelle (my little stepsister, who was adopted from a country called Vietnam), Nannie (my stepgrandmother), Shannon (my stepbrother David Michael's puppy), Boo-Boo (Daddy's meanie cat), Crystal Light the Second (my goldfish), and Goldfishie (Andrew's goldfish). Oh, yes, Moosie, my other stuffed cat is not going to camp either.

They all live at the big house. It is in Stoneybrook, Connecticut, too. Andrew and I live there every other weekend, on some holidays and vacations, and for two weeks during the summer.

I will tell you why I live in two houses. It is because a long time ago Mommy and Daddy got divorced. Then they each married other people and made new families. So Andrew and I have two houses and two families. That is why I call us Karen Two-Two and Andrew Two-Two. (I got the idea for those names when my teacher, Ms. Colman, read my class a book called *Jacob Two-Two Meets the Hooded Fang*.)

Now I will tell you who *is* going to camp with me: Nancy Dawes and Hannie Papadakis. Nancy and Hannie are my best friends. Nancy lives next door to Mommy. Hannie lives across the street from Daddy and one house down. We are all in the same class at Stoneybrook Academy. And we call ourselves the Three Musketeers. That is because we do everything together. (Well, almost everything. The last time we went to camp Hannie could not go. So it was just me and Nancy.)

The other person who is going to camp is David Michael, my stepbrother. He is seven like me. (Well, actually, he is a few months older, which is important to him, but not to me.) David Michael was at camp last time, too. So was Kristy. But she can't come this summer. That is okay. I will miss her, but I will be fine without her.

I know everything there is to know about going to camp. I know about horseback rid-

4

ing, swimming, and hiking. I know about living in a cabin. I know about camp food. And I know about having fun.

If you want to know anything about camp, just ask me. I know it all.

Nancy

Hello. My name is Nancy Dawes. I am seven and three quarters years old. I have long, reddish hair. I have a whole bunch of freckles. And I have hazel eyes. That means they are kind of gray, green, and blue all at the same time.

I live in Stoneybrook, Connecticut, with my mommy, my daddy, my brother, Danny, and my kitten, Pokey.

Only this summer I will live someplace else. I will live at Camp Mohawk for one whole week. I am going there in just two days. Mommy wants me to finish packing today.

"Do you think I should bring my red sweater or my blue sweater? Do you think I should pack two books, or three?" I asked.

I was talking to my brother, Danny. Mommy had set up his playpen in my room. Danny is only a baby. He cannot talk yet. But sometimes I think he answers my questions anyway. That is because I understand him the best. When Danny hiccups, it means yes. When he burps, it means no.

"I wish I could take you to camp with me," I said. "Would you like to go to Camp Mohawk, Danny?"

"Hic! Hic-hic!" Danny hiccupped.

"I knew it! I knew you would want to come with me," I said.

I ran downstairs to find Mommy. She was in the kitchen reading her newspaper.

"Mommy, can Danny come to Camp Mohawk? He wants to. He told me so himself," I said.

7

"I am sure he wants to be with his big sister. But I do not think little babies are allowed at camp," said Mommy.

"I guess you are right," I replied.

"Did you pack your address book? I know Grandma B would like to get a post-card from you," said Mommy.

"I forgot. I will go pack it now," I said.

Grandma B is not my real grandma. But she is just as good as any real grandma could be. She lives at Stoneybrook Manor. A lot of old people live there. I talk to her on the phone. And she comes to visit on important holidays like Rosh Hashanah and Yom Kippur and Passover.

I wonder if Grandma B would like to come to camp with me. She likes to dance and sing and listen to music. But I do not know if she could play softball or go hiking anymore. She is *really* old.

I guess Grandma B and Danny will just have to stay home in Stoneybrook. Sometimes I wish I could stay home, too. I will tell you a secret: I am afraid I am going to be homesick at camp.

But I will be with my two best friends. They are Karen Brewer and Hannie Papadakis. They are both seven, like me. Only Karen is a younger seven than Hannie and me. We are the Three Musketeers. We go to school together. We play together. And now all three of us are going to camp together.

When I went to camp last time, I was just a little bit homesick. But that was before Danny came. Now I am afraid I am going to miss him so, so much. But I am going to camp anyway. That is final.

I found my address book and dropped it into my backpack. Under the address book I found a photo. It showed me holding Danny.

"Look. This is the day you came home from the hospital. Mommy and Daddy let me sit in a chair and hold you. Are you going to miss me, Danny?" I asked.

Danny did not hiccup. He did not burp. He looked at me and blew little spit bubbles. I was sure that meant he would miss me a lot.

I carefully put the picture of Danny and me into one of my books. Then I dropped the book into my pack.

I am glad the Three Musketeers are going to camp together, I thought. If I really do get homesick, I will need my best friends around me.

Hannie

Hey! It's me, Hannie Papadakis. My real and true name is Hannah Papadakis. But no one calls me Hannah, even though it is a neat name. My teacher, Ms. Colman, told me that my name is a palindrome. That means it is exactly the same if you spell it forward or backward.

You might already know from my last name that I am Greek. But I have never been to Greece. I have mostly just been to Stoneybrook, Connecticut. That is where I live.

Here is what I look like. I have dark eyes

11

Hannie

and dark hair. Most of the time I wear my hair in pigtails.

I am seven-going-on-eight. I have a big brother named Linny. He is nine-going-on-ten. He is usually nice. Except when he teases me. My sister, Sari, is two-going-on-three. She is usually a pain in the neck. Except when she is sleeping.

My family has three pets. They are Noodle the Poodle, Pat the Cat, and Myrtle the Turtle. They are nice all the time. Once I thought of a good name for a pet. Plunk. I asked Mommy and Daddy if we could get a skunk since I already had the perfect name for it. But they said no way.

Hey, maybe I will meet a skunk at camp. Did I tell you I am going to camp? Well, I am. I am going tomorrow. Wow!

Linny is going, too. So are my two best friends, Karen Brewer and Nancy Dawes. We always try to stick together. That is why we call ourselves the Three Musketeers. Last time only two Musketeers could go to Camp Mohawk. I could not go. That was sad. But this summer we will be together.

I do not think we should be together every single minute, though. I want to make new friends, too.

"Good night, Hannie," said Linny. He passed my room with a sleeping bag tucked under his arm. "See you in the morning."

"Are you camping out *again*? You have slept in the yard every single night this week," I said.

"Starting tomorrow we are going to have to rough it. And I want to be ready. Camping is not for sissies," said Linny.

Well, I am no sissy. And I was not going to have one bit of trouble at Camp Mohawk.

I was just about to close my camp bag when Sari walked into my room. She put a scruffy pink puppy on top. "Muffin go camp!" said Sari.

I handed the dog right back. "Thanks. But Muffin cannot come to camp. I will be too busy to take care of her," I said.

I will be busy making new friends, playing softball, hiking, and swimming. I just love to swim. Daddy calls me "The Big Fish." This summer I am going to get so good at swimming that I will be ready for the Olympics.

"And the gold medal goes to Hannie 'The Big Fish' Papadakis!" the announcer will say.

I checked my bag one last time. Camp Mohawk, here I come!

KAREN

Good-byes

I woke up in my bed at the little house. It was Saturday. Not just any Saturday. It was Camp Mohawk Saturday.

I got dressed in a hurry. First I put on my underwear. That was the boring part. Then I put on my T-shirt, shorts, and socks. That was the fun part. Everything you wear at Camp Mohawk — except for your underwear and sneakers — has to have a teepee on it. (Kristy says it should have been something called a longhouse because that is what Mohawk Indians lived in. But I like teepees better.)

I looked in the mirror. Too bad I did not have teepee barrettes. Oh, well.

"Karen, breakfast is ready!" called Mommy.

I hurried downstairs. All my favorite things to eat were on the table. Krispy Krunchy Cereal. Scrambled eggs, well done. Rice cakes with cream cheese and jelly. Purple grape juice in my purple cup.

"You said the food wasn't so great at camp. So we made you a special going-away breakfast," said Seth.

"Thank you," I said.

"Are you excited?" asked Mommy.

"Yes," I replied. "But I already know everything that is going to happen to me today. First I will get on the bus. Some of the kids will be shouting out the window. Some of the kids will be crying. Then we will ride up to Lake . . . whatever it's called."

"Lake Dekanawida," said Seth.

16

"Right," I said. "And then Old Meanie — um, Mrs. Means — will tell me which cabin I am in. Then I will meet my counselor. Then we will go to our cabins and unpack."

"And then you will come home?" asked Andrew.

"I will be home in one week," I said.

I ate a little of everything, then asked, "May I be excused now? I have a lot of good-byes to say."

"I'll let you know when it's time to leave," said Mommy.

I ran upstairs to my room. I said good-bye to Goosie, Hyacynthia my china baby doll, and Terry my doll sister (Nancy and Hannie have doll sisters, too).

"Emily Junior, you behave yourself," I said to my rat. "Mommy and Seth will take care of you. If you are very good, they will let you run around in the closet."

When I finished saying good-bye to everyone in my room, I went looking for

17

Rocky and Midgie. I found them curled up together in the living room.

"You two take care of each other," I said. "I know you will miss me very, very much. But don't be too sad. I will be back in a week."

"It's time to go, honey," said Mommy. "Seth will put your bag in the car."

"Good-bye, house!" I called.

We drove to Stoneybrook High School. That is where the camp bus was going to pick me up. The school parking lot was a mess of kids and their families.

I found my big house family right away. I love when my two families get together. Then we are one huge family! (But maybe it is not such a happy family. The grown-ups always look kind of uncomfortable.)

"Hi, Daddy! Hi, everyone!" I called.

The next thing I knew, Hannie and Nancy and their families had joined us.

The Three Musketeers were gigundoly excited. We did our special handshake: We clapped our hands once. We made a tower

18

out of our fists. Then we snapped our fingers twice.

Just as we finished, the bus pulled in. I looked at my great, big family. I had a lot of good-byes to say. (Nancy and Hannie had only three each.) I had to talk fast, or the bus would leave without me.

"Good-bye, Mommy. Good-bye, Daddy," I said. "Good-bye, Seth. Good-bye, Elizabeth."

I hugged and said good-bye to everyone. I saved Kristy's good-bye for last.

"I wish you were coming with me," I whispered to her.

Then I climbed onto the bus.

Nancy

Big Blue Frog

I waved out the window of the camp bus to Mommy, Daddy, and Danny. Mommy was holding up Danny's hand and waving it back to me. My tummy did a few flip-flops when the motor started and we pulled out of the school parking lot.

David Michael was sitting three seats ahead of Karen and Hannie and me. "Camp Mohawk, here we come!" he shouted.

Linny was sitting next to David Michael. "Get that bug juice ready!" he called. (That is what everyone calls the fruit punch at camp.)

Some CITs (those letters stand for Counselor-in-Training) were sitting at the back of the bus. They were mostly girls in Kristy's Baby-sitters Club. I could hear Mallory Pike and Claudia Kishi calling, "Blue frog! Blue frog!" Then other voices joined in. "Blue frog! Blue frog!"

Finally, someone started to sing, *"Oh, I'm in love with a big blue frog, and a big blue frog loves me! It's not as odd as it may seem, he wears glasses and he's six foot three!"*

I was sitting next to Hannie. She was singing the song at the top of her lungs. Karen was, too. I started singing with them.

Only I wasn't singing as loudly. I was still thinking about Danny and Mommy and Daddy. I was missing them.

As soon as the kids finished singing "Big Blue Frog" two times in a row, Karen started a new song.

"There was a farmer had a dog, and Bingo was

his name-o. B-I-N-G-O! B-I-N-G-O! B-I-N-G-O! And Bingo was his name-o!"

The second time around, we clapped instead of singing the letter B. Then we clapped for the letters B and I. We kept going that way until we weren't singing any letters at all. We were just clapping. *Clap, clap, clap-clap-clap! Clap, clap, clap-clap-clap! Clap, clap, clap-clap-clap! "And Bingo was his name-o!"*

When the song ended we heard someone call, "Paper bag! Paper bag!"

This was not the beginning of a new song. It was Margo Pike calling for a paper bag because she was about to be sick. Her sister, Mallory, raced to the front of the bus with the bag. She reached Margo just in time.

I wondered if being bus-sick felt as bad as being homesick. Suddenly Hannie was whispering something in my ear.

"That tickles!" I cried.

"We're playing Telephone," said Hannie. "Now you have to whisper to Becca."

22

Becca Ramsey was in the seat in front of me.

"Say the sentence again," I said. "I didn't hear it."

Hannie whispered the sentence to me again. Then I whispered it to Becca. This was the sentence: *Camp Mohawk campers have big fun.*

Becca whispered it to Charlotte Johanssen, her best friend. Charlotte whispered it to David Michael. David Michael whispered it to Linny.

By the time the sentence reached the front of the bus, it sounded like this: *Most good campers weigh a ton!*

Do you know what? I laughed so hard, I forgot all about being homesick.

Hannie

Cabin 7-A

"We're here because we're here because we're here because we're here! We're here because they drove us here. We're here because we're here!"

That was the last song we sang on the camp bus. As usual, Karen and I were singing at the top of our lungs. (Nancy was being kind of quiet.)

The girls piled off the bus. Linny and the other boys stayed on. That is because the boys' camp was at the other side of Lake, um, Lake — I forget the name. I waved good-bye to Linny and jumped off the bus.

"Attention all campers, counselors, and CITs. Please assemble for cabin assignments," said a voice over the loudspeaker.

"That's Old Meanie — I mean Mrs. Means. She's our camp director," explained Karen.

We followed everyone to a big, open area around a flagpole. The Three Musketeers linked arms and listened as Mrs. Means read off the cabin assignments.

"In Cabin 7-A, the counselor will be Rikki Morse," said Mrs. Means. "The CITs are Megan Robbins and Jody Stein. The campers are as follows."

She called out the names of six girls, who were all seven years old. (Cabin 7-A. Seven-year-olds. Get it?) I heard Nancy's name. Then my name. But I did not hear Karen's name. I wondered if I had missed it.

"In Cabin 7-B, the counselor will be Nora Geller," continued Mrs. Meanie. "The CITs are Betsy Pink and Mary Lowell. The campers are as follows."

Karen's name was the first one called.

The Three Musketeers were not going to be in the same cabin. Oh, well. Karen said the A and B cabins were connected. We would still get to see each other a lot. But we would not have to be together every second. And there would be one more girl in my cabin who I did not already know. One more new girl to make friends with.

We walked to the cabins together. Karen was busy introducing herself to everyone in sight.

"See you later!" she called to Nancy and me.

Nancy and I went into our cabin and found an empty bunk. I wanted the one right in the middle, so I could see everything that was going on. Nancy let me have the top. I climbed up and tried it on for size. Perfect.

"Hey, Hannie. I see an empty bed," said Nancy. She sounded excited. "Karen can sleep there!"

"But she is not in our cabin," I said.

"She can switch. Then the Three Mus-

27

keteers can be together!" said Nancy.

Just then a girl came in, dragging her bag behind her. Nancy looked disappointed.

"Maybe that girl will switch with Karen," whispered Nancy. "Or maybe Old Meanie got the names mixed up. Let's go ask her."

I did not even bother to answer Nancy. She was acting like a dweeb. I climbed down from my bed and started to unpack.

"Hi, everyone," said Rikki, our counselor. "Let's take a break from unpacking to introduce ourselves. When I point to you, tell us your name, where you come from, and one important thing you would like us to know about you."

I listened as my bunkies introduced themselves. Jill Locke was from Pennsylvania. She was learning to play the guitar. Amy Berke was from New York City. She wants to be a stand-up comic someday. Sophie Harris was from Connecticut and rides horses. Christine Sklar was from New Jersey. This was her first time at sleep-away camp.

28

When it was Nancy's turn, she told everyone that she was from Stoneybrook, Connecticut, and has a new baby brother named Danny. "I wish I did not have to leave him at home," she added.

Then it was my turn.

"My name is Hannie Papadakis," I said. "I am from Stoneybrook, Connecticut. And this week I want to make a lot of new friends!"

DAVID MICHAEL

Wilson the Wimp

I'm here because I'm here because I'm here.

And boy am I glad!

Our camp director, Mr. Means, just finished giving us our cabin assignments. Linny Papadakis was in Cabin 9-A. That is because he is nine. (Cabin 9-A. Nine-year-olds. Get it?)

"See you around, David Michael," called Linny.

"See you," I called back.

I was in Cabin 7-A. (Guess how old I am.) I did not know any of the kids in my cabin yet. No problem. Being on my own was going to be fun. You don't get to be on your own very much when you come from a family as big as mine. (There are ten of us, counting Karen and Andrew, but not counting the pets.)

This summer I am going to be Independent with a capital I. At home I have enough little brothers and sisters to look after. And enough grown-ups looking after *me*.

My counselor's name was Rick Lyon. Last year he was a CIT in this cabin. He is pretty wild. But Mr. Means must like him. Everyone in camp has to wear a tee-pee T-shirt. But Rick gets to wear another shirt on top. It has pictures of bowling balls and bowling pins all over it. It is wild.

After we introduced ourselves, Rick made an announcement.

"This summer, the seven-year-olds are going to be part of an experiment," he said. "Each of you is going to be assigned a 'little brother' from one of the six-year-old cabins. How about that?"

How about that? How about sending me home! I came to camp to get away from little kids. I have all the little brothers and sisters I need back where I came from.

"Yo, David Michael. Are you with us?" asked Rick.

"Huh?" I said.

"Your little brother is going to be Wilson Tenney. He is in Cabin 6-B," said Rick. "We'll head over to the sixes as soon as everyone finishes unpacking."

I tried unpacking really, really slowly. But it did not do any good. I had to leave when everyone else was ready anyway.

The kids in Cabin 6-B were wearing name tags. As soon as I saw Wilson Tenney, I knew I was in trouble. All I could think was Wimp with a capital W.

I had to introduce myself to him anyway.

"Hi," I said. "I'm David Michael, your big brother."

"Achoo!" said Wilson. He wiped his runny nose with the back of his hand.

"Maybe you need a handkerchief or something," I said. I was trying to act like a big brother. I was also trying not to gag.

"I — ah-ah-*choo*! — have allergies," said Wilson, sniffling. "I am allergic to pollen, dust — *achoo!* — every animal you can name, and most of the activities they are going to make me do while I am here."

Oh, brother! Just what I needed. I was glad I did not have to be Wilson's pal all day long. Rick said we only had to spend one hour a day with our little brothers.

Still a whole hour! I did not even want to spend one second with this kid.

"Okay, everyone. It's time to say good-

bye. But we'll be having a campfire sing-along tonight. You will get to sit with your little brothers then," said Rick.

I needed a plan. Let me see. I could sit down next to Wilson. The minute he sneezed I could tell him he was allergic to me. Then I would do him a big favor and disappear. Forever.

KAREN

Karen the Know-It-All

"Good night, Sasha, Corinne, Janet, Becky, and Maggie!" I called to my bunkies.

It was lights out for Cabin 7-B.

"I wonder what time we have to wake up tomorrow," said Janet.

"I can tell you exactly what time," I said. "Old Meanie will wake us up at seven sharp. I know what she will say, too. She will say, 'GOOD MORNING, CAMPERS, COUNSELORS, AND CITs. TODAY IS SUNDAY. BREAKFAST WILL BE SERVED IN HALF AN HOUR. THE MENU IS WAF-

FLES, BACON, AND ORANGE JUICE. HAVE A NICE DAY!' "

"Thank you and good night, Karen," said Nora, our counselor.

"You are very welcome," I replied. "Good night."

The next morning, we were up at seven sharp, just like I said. The only difference was Mrs. Meanie announced that we were having pancakes instead of waffles.

The kids from all the cabins walk to the mess hall together, so I got to see Hannie and Nancy.

Nancy gave me a gigundoly big hug. She acted as if she had not seen me for a hundred years.

"Hi, Karen!" cried Hannie. "I loved my first night of camp. It was so much fun."

The Three Musketeers marched arm in arm to the mess hall. We sang "John Jacob Jingleheimer Schmidt" as loudly as we could the whole way.

When we got inside, I heard a girl behind me say, "I hope there is something for me to eat besides pancakes. Pancakes give me a bellyache."

"Do not worry," I said. "You just have to ask Old Meanie for a substitute. You can have eggs or cereal. When you are an old camper like me, you know these things."

After breakfast we went back to our cabins to straighten up. Then it was time for swimming.

"I wonder if the water will be cold," said Maggie.

"The water is really, really cold. But you forget all about it once you start moving around," I explained. "You have to be careful when you get in, though. Some parts of the lake are rocky. I will show you. And you have to wear shoes on the dock, or you could get a splinter. And don't forget your swimming cap or the counselor will send you back. And . . ."

"Thank you very much, Karen," said Nora.

Guess what. When we reached the lake,

Corinne had to go all the way back to the cabin because she had forgotten her cap. I wanted to say, "I told you so." But I did not. I did not want to act like a know-it-all.

After swimming, Nora told us we would be going on a hike in the afternoon.

"I am sure Karen can tell you all about hiking," she added.

"That is right!" I said. "I know how to follow a trail. You just have to look for the cairns. They are piles of stones that mark the way. And I know how to use a compass. All you need to know is that it always points north. I know because I went hiking before."

"I am afraid we are boring you at camp this summer, Karen," said Nora. "Let me see. Maybe we can find something that would be new and exciting for you. Tell me, did you go on any overnight trips when you were here last time?"

"No," I replied. "But I went camping once with my family."

"Well, we will be going on a campout this Thursday night, before we go home," said Nora. "Do you think you would like that?"

"Sure," I replied. "I know some kids get scared camping out. But not me. I love camping!"

Nancy

Homesick

I looked at the clock beside my bunk. It was six-thirty. In half an hour Old Meanie would wake us up.

I missed my alarm clock at home. It looks like a cat. It wakes me up by saying, "Meow, meow, meow." That is much nicer than Old Meanie shouting over the loudspeaker.

The night had lasted forever and ever. In the middle of the night I had had to go to the bathroom. The bathroom is all the way in the back of the cabin and there is no light in it. I am afraid of going to the bathroom in the dark. So I woke up my counselor, Rikki, and asked her to go with me. She did not seem very happy. After that I could not fall asleep again.

I knew I would be homesick. I just knew it. I miss Mommy and Daddy and Danny and Pokey. I miss Grandma B. I miss my clock and my dolls and the bathroom with the night light and soft seat.

Camp is too rough for me. There are bugs. I do not like the food. We are busy every single minute. We hardly ever just sit.

The Three Musketeers are not even together. Karen is in another cabin. She does things at different times from me and Hannie. And Hannie is always running around. She wants to do everything. She wants to meet everyone. She hardly has any time for me. I am lonely here.

"GOOD MORNING, CAMPERS, COUNSELORS, AND CITs. TODAY IS SUNDAY. BREAKFAST WILL BE . . ."

"Hurry up and get dressed, Hannie," I said. "Karen will be waiting outside."

"Go ahead," said Hannie, yawning. "I'll meet you."

By the time I was dressed and ready to go, Hannie was still in her pajamas, brushing her teeth. That is because she was busy talking to the other bunkies.

I ran outside to see if Karen was there yet. She was!

"Hi, Karen!" I called. I gave her a great, big hug.

When Hannie finally came out, the Three Musketeers linked arms and headed for the mess hall. We sang "John Jacob Jingleheimer Schmidt." Then Karen sat with her bunkies and we sat with ours.

I sat next to Christine. She's kind of quiet, but nice. I could tell she did not like camp food either. She hardly ate anything.

After breakfast, we had clean-up, then volleyball, then swimming. Karen was on her way back from the lake, when we were on our way down. She waved and called, "I'm going horseback riding! See you at dinner!"

I wish the Three Musketeers could stay together. I know I would feel better.

"Good morning, swimmers," said Hank, the swimming instructor. "Everyone into the water for warm-up. Then get ready for a relay race."

"I am swimming faster every day!" said Hannie.

She jumped right into the water. I stayed behind on the dock. I hate the way the bottom of the lake feels. It is covered with rocks and slippery weeds. One time I felt something long and wiggly. I am sure it was a snake.

"Hey, Hannie," I called when she swam by me. "Stay with me on the dock. Please?"

"I can't. It's almost time for the race," said Hannie. She grabbed a kickboard and kicked across to the rope on the other side.

I was the only one who was not in the water. Well, almost the only one. Christine

was halfway in. She took two steps forward. Then three steps back. Forward. Back. Finally she turned and came back to the dock.

She sat down next to me. "I thought I felt a snake," she said. "I'm afraid of snakes."

"Me, too," I said. "But I think we're safe here."

Nature Boy

Cabins? Bunks? I thought I was going to be roughing it. I may as well be at home in my bed.

Camp is okay so far. I am in Cabin 9-A. That is because I am nine years old. (9-A. Nine years old. Get it?)

I get to play volleyball, softball, and basketball. And I go swimming every day. (You should see my sister, Hannie. She's turning into a really cool swimmer.)

"Come on, Linny. We don't want to be

late for supper. Burgers and bug juice," said my bunkie, Jimmy.

Burgers? Bug juice? I thought I was going to be hunting for food in the woods. Catching fish. Picking berries. Instead we eat in a mess hall. I may as well be eating in the school cafeteria.

One good thing, though. Mr. Means, the boys' camp director, said we were going on an overnight on Thursday. Today is Monday. Three more days until camping out. At least I'll get to live out in the wild for one night.

After dinner we went to the rec hall to see a movie called *Meatballs*. It is a goofy comedy about a bunch of kids at Camp Sasquatch. They didn't rough it there either. Doesn't anybody rough it at camp?

I couldn't wait to get back to the bunk for lights out. As soon as it was quiet, I did what I've been doing every night since I got to Camp Mohawk. I sneaked out of bed. I rolled up a sheet and put it under my blanket. I bunched it up so it would look like I

49

was still curled up there. Then I slipped outside.

I found the blanket I had stashed behind the cabin. The air was cold. But I didn't mind. That is what camping out is all about. Coming face to face with nature. Roughing it.

I wrapped myself up in the blanket to keep warm, just the way I had done every night since I got here. Then I settled down under a tree to get some sleep.

Before I closed my eyes, I gazed up at the stars. I found the North Star, the Big Dipper, and the Little Dipper.

I was just about to doze off, when I heard a voice say, "Back to bed, Nature Boy." (That is what everyone calls me.) "You know you can't sleep out here."

It was my counselor, Rob. He had come out to find me. Just the way he had every night since I got here.

Oh, well. On Thursday night I would be able to sleep outside. And no one would come drag me back in.

50

Hannie

The Big Fight

It was Tuesday morning. Sports Day!

Nancy and I and our bunkies were on the blue team. Old Meanie (she's not really so mean) hung blue streamers outside our cabin.

Karen and her bunkies were on the red team. (They got red streamers.)

At breakfast, our table was set with blue napkins and a blue flag. We had pancakes with blueberries. Karen's bunk had red napkins, a red flag, and strawberries.

51

Hannie

I don't care what anyone says. I think the food here is great. But, then, I think *everything* about Camp Mohawk is great.

The first event was swimming. I jumped into the water for warm-up. Karen was busy complaining about how boring relay races are. And Nancy stayed behind on the dock. I heard her tell the counselor she did not feel good. But I do not think she was telling the truth.

"Everyone line up for the race," called Hank, the swimming instructor.

I hurried out of the water and waited for the whistle. As soon as I heard it, I flew back in. I raced to the rope and back as fast as I could swim (which is really fast). I tagged my bunkie, Jill. Jill swam to the rope and back, then tagged Amy. Amy swam to the rope, then came back and tagged the wall.

"Blue team!" she called.

The blue team was jumping up and

down, shouting, "We won! We won!"

"Congratulations," said Nancy. "Do you want to sit with me? We don't have to go to softball yet."

"No, thanks. The elevens are playing basketball," I said. "I want to cheer them on."

"Can't you stay here for one minute?" said Nancy. She grabbed my T-shirt and hung on to it.

"Do you mind?" I asked. "I am going up to watch basketball. You are welcome to come if you want."

I left Nancy on the dock, moping. I ran back to the cabin to change out of my wet bathing suit. Then I went to the basketball court with Amy and Jill.

"Go, blue, go! Go, blue, go!" we cheered.

We must have done a good job cheering. The blue team won!

Our counselor, Rikki, was giving us the softball line-up when Nancy came dawdling

ill. She looked kind of lost.

"Are you going to play softball with us?"
I asked.

"Old Meanie says I have to," said Nancy.

"Gee, you could try having a little team
spirit," I replied.

Nancy was assigned the outfield. She
stood there looking dreamy. In the third
inning, the ball headed in her direction. The
bases were loaded. But Nancy just stood
there. I could not believe it. By the time
she had run after the ball and thrown it, all
four red team players had slid into home
base.

Guess what. We lost the game.

It was time for lunch. I walked to the
mess hall with Jill. We were singing "John
Jacob Jingleheimer Schmidt" when Nancy
caught up with us.

"I thought that was the Three Musketeers' song," said Nancy.

"It's just a song. Anyone is allowed to
sing it, you know," I replied.

"Will you sit next to me at lunch, Han-

54

nie?" asked Nancy. She was hanging on to my T-shirt again. That did it.

"Just leave me alone already!" I cried.

Karen was ahead of us with her bunkies. She turned around to look at me.

I did not say another word to Nancy. I stomped off to the mess hall with Jill. Jill, who was *not* hanging on to my shirt.

KAREN

Bor-ing!

It was Tuesday. Sports Day. Yawn.

My cabin was on the red team. Hannie and Nancy's cabin was on the blue. Our first event was a swimming relay race. We had a relay race yesterday. *Bor-ing!*

Nancy had the right idea. She told the counselor she did not feel good.

"Do I have to be in the relay race? I am so, so tired. And relay races are so, so bor-ing," I said to Hank, our swimming instructor.

"Put on your cap, Karen Brewer," said

56

Hank. "The race is about to start and we need you."

I stood at the edge of the dock. The whistle blew. Hannie flew into the water. I put my big toe in to see how cold it was. It was pretty cold, but everyone was yelling at me to jump. So finally I did.

Hannie was on her second lap, and I was starting my first.

"Hurry, Karen, hurry!" called my bunkies.

I wanted to tell them I was moving as fast as I could. But if I opened my mouth I would get a mouthful of Lake . . . Whatever . . . water.

Can you believe it? Everyone blamed me when we lost.

Boring-ball, I mean softball, was next. My counselor, Nora, made me the catcher. She thought that would keep me awake. It did. Most of the game.

I dozed off once or twice. Nancy was dozing in the outfield. She missed a really important play. Thanks to her, my team won.

After the game, I headed up to the mess hall with my bunkies. All of a sudden, I heard someone shout, "Just leave me alone already!" It was Hannie. She was fighting with Nancy. She stomped away, leaving Nancy behind.

"What is going on?" I asked. "Are you mad at Nancy for missing the ball?"

"No. Everyone makes mistakes. I am mad at Nancy because she is hanging all over me. She does not want me to swim. She does not want me to be with my new friends. She does not want me to do anything without her."

"Come on, Karen!" called Maggie. "We're waiting."

I wanted to talk to Hannie and Nancy. I wanted to help. But I could not desert my bunkies.

"See you later. I hope you and Hannie make up soon," I said.

I went into the mess hall.

"What's for lunch?" I asked Sasha.

"Tuna salad sandwiches. Jell-O for dessert," she replied.

"*Bor-ing!*" I shouted. "Capital B-O-R-I-N-G, boring!"

"That is enough, K-A-R-E-N," said Nora.

I was b-o-r-e-d the rest of the day. Only I did not say so out loud. At lights out, Nora came to visit me in my bunk. She wanted us to have a talk.

"Karen, if you don't mind my saying so, I think you have a little bit of an attitude problem," she said.

"Maybe I do. You see, I have done all this before," I said. "When my sister was here."

"Well, we have something special planned for Thursday," said Nora. "Our cabin and Cabin 7-A will be leaving the campgrounds to go to a state fair."

"Really?" I said. "That is not boring at all!"

"And Thursday night is our campout," added Nora.

I was about to say *bor-ing* when Nora

said, "I have decided that you should have the honor of planning some special features for the campout. That should keep you from getting *too* bored. Don't you think so?"

"I know so," I replied. Hmm. What could I plan for the campout that would be really special and not one bit boring?

I did not know the answer right away. But I knew I would think of something. I always do.

DAVID MICHAEL
Boo!

"It's your turn, David Michael," said my counselor, Rick.

We were practicing telling a ghost story. It was Wednesday. After supper the whole camp was going to gather around a campfire. The kids in my cabin and Cabin 7-B were going to take turns telling the story.

I stood up and said my lines, *"There once lived a teeny tiny man. One day the teeny tiny man put on a teeny tiny hat and went out of his teeny tiny house to take a teeny tiny walk."*

The next thing that happens is that the teeny tiny man goes to a teeny tiny grave-yard and finds a teeny tiny bone. When he takes the bone home, it starts talking to him.

That story did not scare me. And I did not think it would scare anyone else either. Except maybe for little kids who did not know it already. I was afraid my bunkies and I would look like dweebs at the campfire.

"Time for supper, kids," said Rick, when we finished practicing.

We headed for the mess hall. As soon as we got inside, my little brother, Wilson, spotted me. He was smiling like crazy. And waving. (At least he was not sneezing. I think he got allergy pills at the infirmary.)

After supper, the sevens had to walk with their little brothers, the sixes, to Mo-hawk Meadow. That was where the camp-fire was going to be.

Wilson was all excited about it. But I was not.

"What's the matter?" asked Wilson.

"Nothing," I said. "Nothing a little six-year-old could help with."

"Tell me anyway," said Wilson.

I knew I shouldn't, but I did. I told Wilson what was bothering me.

"The sevens are telling a ghost story and it's hardly even scary," I said.

"I can help you with that," replied Wilson, smiling.

Yeah, right, I thought.

When we reached Mohawk Meadow, my stepsister, Karen, called, "Hi, David Michael! I am going to sing a spooky song with my bunkies. What are you going to do?"

"We're telling a story," I mumbled. "See you later."

I sat down by the campfire with the rest of the kids. I hoped Mr. and Mrs. Means would forget about us. Or maybe they would run out of time.

No such luck.

"And now we will hear a scary story told

by the boys in Cabins 7-A and 7-B," said Mr. Means.

"Okay, David Michael," whispered Rick. "You're on."

"Once there was a teeny tiny man. One day the teeny tiny man . . ."

Suddenly, a girl screamed, "Eeek!"

I could not understand it. The story was not scary. Especially not the first line. I kept going.

"The teeny tiny man put on a teeny tiny hat . . ."

"Ahhh!" yelled a couple of boys behind me. I stopped until it was quiet again. Then I continued.

"He went out of his teeny tiny house . . ."

"Yeow!!" More and more kids were screaming. I must have been doing a really good job of sounding scary. I finished saying my part in a loud and shivery voice.

"To take a teeny tiny walk!" I said.

"Ooooh!" screamed the Three Musketeers.

When I sat down, kids were still scream-

ing. Boy, was I proud. They screamed through the whole story. At the end, someone yelled "BOO!" The kids went wild.

I wondered who yelled "Boo!" Then I found out. It was my little brother, Wilson. He was the one who was scaring everyone during the story. While we were telling our story, he was poking kids from behind with a long stick.

Hmm. Maybe I had not been fair to my little brother. I decided Wilson was not such a wimp after all.

14

Hannie

Help!

"Step right up! Toss a penny in the bowl and win a prize!" called a lady in a big straw hat.

It was Thursday. Cabins 7-A and 7-B had just piled off the camp bus. We were at the state fair.

"Hey, Hannie, this is cool!" said Karen. She did not seem bored at all. She seemed more like herself again.

Nancy looked lost as usual. But I did not care. I was still not talking to Nancy.

"Mmm, I smell doughnuts," said my

bunkie, Jill. "Maybe I will get one later. And some lemonade, too."

"Okay, girls," said Rikki. "Here's the plan. You may look at the exhibits and animals first. Then we will take a break to buy lunch. After lunch, you can use your spending money on games and rides."

We split up into groups. Thank goodness I was not with Nancy. My group was Jill, Amy, and our CIT, Jody.

"Where should we go first?" asked Amy.

"Let's look at the animals," I suggested.

We started with the cows. I never knew there were so many different kinds — we counted seven kinds at the fair. I liked the Jersey cows best. That is because I have been to New Jersey.

There were lots of goats and sheep, too. We watched one sheep get shaved. I felt sorry for him. He looked sad without his coat.

"Look!" exclaimed Amy. "Those pigs are acting like . . . like pigs!"

The pigs were rolling in the mud.

"They do that to stay cool," explained Jody.

We left the farm animal tent and walked along the midway.

"Oh, wow, these vegetables are wild," I exclaimed. "This tomato looks just like a pear. And here's a pepper that is shaped like the state of Florida."

I wanted to see all the funny vegetables. I walked a little farther into the tent. I wondered if I would find a pumpkin like the one Karen and I entered in the Halloween contest last year. It was shaped just like a cat.

I did not find any pumpkins. But I saw a tomato that was almost the size of a pumpkin.

"Hey, you guys! Look at this!" I cried.

I turned around to look for my friends. They were not behind me. I turned around and around looking for anyone I knew. I did not see a single familiar face.

Uh-oh, I thought. I am lost.

15

Nancy

New Friends, Old Friends

Hannie and I had a bad fight on Tuesday. Well, really, Hannie had the fight by herself. All I did was stand there.

I do not know why she got so mad at me. She yelled, "Leave me alone!" But the Three Musketeers hardly ever leave each other alone. We stick together. At least we used to. Before we came to camp and Karen got put in another cabin and Hannie made so many new friends.

It is Thursday now. I have been at camp for five whole days. I still feel homesick.

But not so much as before. And I am trying harder to be more independent.

"Hey look, Nancy. I can see a Ferris wheel from here. And a roller coaster ride, too," said Christine.

We were sitting together on the bus going to the state fair. Christine was my new camp friend.

"I hope we are in the same group," I said, when Rikki, our counselor, started reading off the names.

I did not want to be in a group with Hannie. Hannie was still not talking to me.

"Nancy, Sophie, and Christine, you will be in Megan's group. Hannie, Amy, and Jill, you will be in Jody's group," said Rikki.

Hurray! Christine was in my group. Sophie was nice. And I was not with Hannie. Today was going to be fun.

"Let's go to the crafts booth, okay?" I suggested.

"Okay," agreed Christine and Sophie.

"And let's be sure to stick together," said

Megan. "I don't want anyone getting lost at the fair."

We held hands as we walked through the crafts tent. We saw a lot of great things. We saw handmade rag dolls, piggy banks, and pretty blankets. I wanted to buy everything I saw.

Christine wanted to see the farm animals next.

"Can you believe how gigantic that hog is!" said Christine.

"I would not like to go grocery shopping for him. It would take a hundred years!" I said.

"And you could not invite him to your house. He would break all the chairs," said Sophie.

We were laughing so hard, we were getting bellyaches.

"Come on, girls," said Megan suddenly. "One of the campers is lost. We have to help find her."

"Who is it?" I asked.

"It's Hannie," replied Megan.

73

Oh, no. Hannie had yelled at me and she was mad at me. But she was still a Musketeer. I had to help find her.

We walked through the midway. That is when I saw the vegetable tent. I remembered how much Hannie liked that cat-shaped pumpkin she and Karen entered in the Halloween contest.

"Megan, we have to go this way. I think Hannie might be in here," I said.

We ran into the tent. It did not take us long to find her. We spotted Hannie all the way at the other end. She was turning around and around. She looked scared.

"Hannie! Hannie! Over here!" I called.

As soon as Hannie heard me calling her, she raced over and gave me the biggest hug ever.

"I knew you would be here. I just knew it. I bet you were looking for a cat pumpkin, right?" I asked.

"How did you know?" said Hannie.

"Because I am a Musketeer. Musketeers know these things about each other."

74

"Oh, Nancy, I am so sorry I yelled at you," said Hannie. "It is good to have new friends. But there is nothing like old friends."

She hugged me again.

"You found her! You found her!" cried Karen, running into the tent. She started hugging us, too. Soon, everyone in Cabins 7-A and 7-B was in one giant circle hug. We were jumping up and down, giggling. All of us — new friends and old.

16

Linny

Nature Boy's Campout

I was finally going to camp out. It probably would not be a *real* campout. But at least I would get to sleep in a tent in a sleeping bag.

It was late in the afternoon on Thursday. Everyone in camp was going on an overnight. Of course the little kids were not going too far from their cabins. But us older kids were going way into the woods.

"Grab your backpacks, guys," said Rob. "We're heading out."

"Are you happy now, Nature Boy?" asked Jimmy.

"Well, it's better than sleeping in the cabin. But it probably won't be a *real* campout anyway," I said.

"It may be more real than you think," said Rob. For some reason, he had a funny grin on his face.

Cabins 9-A and 9-B hiked into the woods. We hiked pretty far. That was a good sign. When we finally stopped, Pete, the counselor in 9-B, made an announcement.

"We decided to make this campout a challenge since you kids are not babies. We brought exactly three matches. That means you better start a fire the old-fashioned way. Save the matches for an emergency. And we won't be having any mess hall sandwiches. We will cook real food. We have fish and rice and a couple of sticks of butter. How's that for a real campout, Nature Boy?" said Pete.

"Great!" I said. I dropped my backpack and got busy.

Linny

I had wanted us to eat only food you could find in the woods. We could have caught the fish in Lake . . . Lake . . . oh, who cares. So fish was okay. But not rice.

I knew we could find better food in the woods if we tried.

"Hey, you guys, let's go see what there is to eat around here," I said.

We went on a food hunt. I was the leader. We found a raspberry bush. Everyone picked a hatful of ripe berries. Growing by the lake we found watercress.

"Yuck!"said Mike, one of the kids in 9-B. "This stuff tastes terrible."

"It will be better when we cook it. Anyway, we're roughing it. We are all going to eat it," I said.

I took charge of making the fire. I started by rubbing two rocks together. I made some sparks but they didn't catch fire.

"Don't worry. Remember, we do have those three matches," said Pete.

"I will not need them," I said confidently. I kept on rubbing till I made a fire.

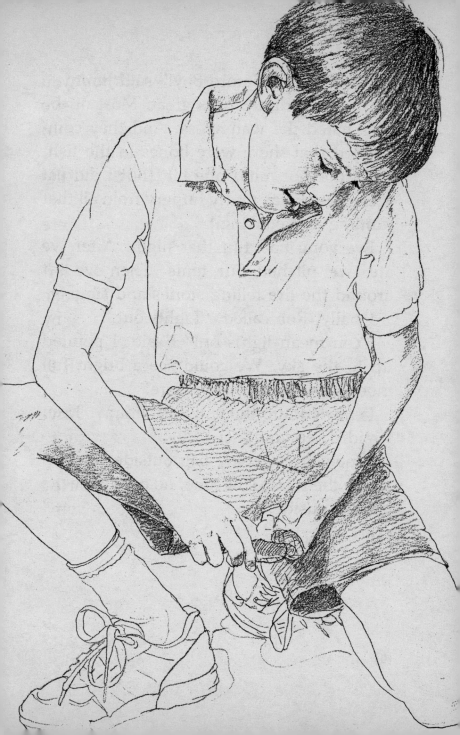

Linny

"Way to go, Nature Boy!" said Jimmy.

I thought dinner was great. Most of the kids hated the watercress. And they complained that there were bones in the fish. But I did not mind one bit. (But I did eat some rice. I was pretty hungry from all that hunting and cooking.)

Everyone had fun that night. After we ate, we pitched our tents. Then we sat around the fire telling stories and singing.

Finally, Rob called, "Lights out."

"You mean lights on!" I said. I pointed up to the sky. We could see a bright full moon—and stars everywhere.

I crawled into the tent with Jimmy. Then I said, "See you later."

I took my sleeping bag outside to sleep under the stars. This time, no one made me go back inside.

Nancy

The Three Musketeers

Hannie got lost at the fair and I found her. Now she is not mad at me anymore. She even apologized for yelling at me.

The Three Musketeers were very happy to be back together again. The counselors let us stick together for the rest of the fair.

When we returned to camp, though, Karen had to go to her cabin. We had to get ready for our campout.

"Sweat shirt!" called Hannie.

"Sweat shirt," the rest of us called back.

It was my turn. We were playing a packing game. One of us called out something to put in the packs and the rest of us repeated it.

"Two pairs of socks!" I said.

"Two pairs of socks," everyone called back.

The game was Rikki's idea. She said no one would forget anything that way.

When we finished, we met Karen and her bunkies outside.

"Usually the sevens camp right over there," said Nora, pointing to a clearing behind the cabins. "But Karen helped us plan this campout, so we're going a little farther into the woods."

"That's right," said Karen. "Staying behind the cabins would have been boring and babyish. Our campout is going to be exciting and fun!"

"All right, everyone, let's go," said Rikki, leading the way.

Some of the kids started singing a marching song. But not Karen. She was yawning and dragging her feet. "Marching songs are boring," she announced.

After losing Hannie at the fair, the Three Musketeers had made a pact to stick together. So Hannie and I had to drag along behind everyone else just to be with Karen.

After we had been walking a long, long time, Karen hurried ahead of us to catch up with her counselor, Nora. She looked a little nervous. "Are we almost there yet?" she asked. "How far away are we?"

That Karen. There is just no pleasing her sometimes. She did not want to camp behind the cabins because that was too close. Now she did not want to go into the woods because it was too far.

I felt like saying something. But I did not. I did not want the Three Musketeers to have another fight. I did want Karen to stop yawning and acting bored, though.

"Psst! Hey, Hannie. Hey, Christine. I have an idea," I whispered. "Let's scare Karen."

Nancy

"How?" asked Christine.

"I saw you pack something you did not call out, Hannie," I said. "I saw you pack a rubber snake."

"I knew it would come in handy," giggled Hannie.

Finally we reached our camp. I called Karen away to look at a bug (there really was no bug), and Hannie slipped the rubber snake under Karen's backpack.

You should have heard Karen scream.

"AHHH!" she yelled. Then she burst into tears.

I felt a little bad. I did not think Karen would be that scared.

"It was only a joke," I said.

"But what if a *real* snake comes to the campsite?" asked Karen. "What do we do then?"

"Time for supper, everyone!" called Rikki.

I could tell Karen did not feel much like eating.

18

Hannie

Hot Dogs and S'mores

Thanks to Karen, we did not have to take picnic baskets with mess hall food on our campout.

Before we left, I heard Karen say to Old Meanie, "That would be too, too boring!"

She begged her to let us have a cookout instead. You know what? Old Meanie was not so mean. She said yes.

So this is what we were going to eat: hot dogs, corn-on-the-cob, and s'mores for dessert.

We had two jobs to do. One was to gather

up sticks for our fire. The other was to take the husks off the corn, then wrap the corn in foil.

Rikki and Nora made the fire and cooked the corn. Then each counselor or CIT helped two kids, and we got to roast our own hot dogs.

"Not too close, Hannie," said Jody. "Nancy, I think you need a longer stick."

Finally we finished cooking and started eating. Everything was delicious.

"This is the best meal I ever ate!" I said.

The s'mores were perfectly sweet and sticky. (In case you do not know it, s'mores are chocolate-covered graham crackers with a marshmallow in the middle, cooked over the fire.) I was still scraping marshmallow off my face when it started to get dark.

Suddenly, I saw something moving overhead. It was swooping back and forth. Back and forth.

"Look, everybody. I think I see a bat up there," I said.

We looked up and saw *lots* of bats. Ooh, spooky.

"Now, let me see," said Rikki. "Here are the things Karen suggested we do tonight. Play Murder-in-the-Dark — "

"No!" said Karen. "I changed my mind. Let's just sing songs."

"But we always do that," said Rikki.

"Let's tell ghost stories!" said Sasha.

"We always do that, too," said Rikki. "Karen wanted — "

"Ghost stories! Ghost stories!" chanted the girls.

"I know a great one!" I cried.

It was completely dark now, except for the moon and the stars and the light of the fire. And the woods were quiet, except for the rustling of the leaves in the wind, and the chirping of the insects.

I took my flashlight out of my backpack and held it up to my face. I wanted to look as scary as could be. Then, in a deep and creepy voice, I began to tell my story.

"Once upon a time, on a dark, dark

89

Hannie

night, in a dark, dark house, a man sat in a rocking chair and rocked. Creak, creak went the chair. Suddenly, there came a knock at the door.''

I looked at the faces around the campfire. Everyone was listening. They were waiting for me to go on. So I did. I told my scary story.

KAREN

Karen, the Scaredy-Cat

If it were not for me, we would be camping in Mohawk Meadow, like the little kids. From Mohawk Meadow you can see the mess hall, the infirmary, Old Meanie's office, everything. Thanks to me we were camping out in the woods.

"Hey, Karen. You are going to walk with us, aren't you?" said Nancy. "The Three Musketeers have to stick together."

I was glad Hannie and Nancy were talking again.

"All right, everyone, let's go," said Rikki.

We left the campgrounds and walked into the woods. I felt as if we were walking forever. I started getting a funny feeling in my stomach. It was a nervous butterfly feeling. I decided I did not like being in the woods.

The more we walked the worse I felt. I was glad when we finally reached the campsite. We dropped our backpacks and started looking around.

"Hey, Karen, come here a minute. There is an amazing bug I want to show you," called Nancy, pointing to a log.

I bent over the log. "What bug?" I said. "I do not see any bug."

"Oh, it must have crawled away," said Nancy.

So I started unpacking.

Suddenly, I screamed, *"AUGHHH!"* A snake was under my backpack.

Hannie, Nancy, Christine, and the other kids were laughing. It turned out to be Hannie's rubber snake.

I knew my friends were just trying to be

funny. But that snake scared me. What if a real snake came along?

We ate hot dogs and corn and s'mores for dinner. But I could not eat much. I was not hungry.

By the time we finished it was dark. Bats were flying all over the place. I started thinking about how far we were from our cabins.

Then Hannie told a ghost story. It was so scary that I screamed again. I could not help it.

"Come on, Karen. Don't be such a scaredy-cat," said Becky.

I did not want my bunkies to think I was a baby, so I shut my mouth and did not scream again.

Finally, Rikki said, "Time for bed, girls. We are heading back to camp early tomorrow."

"Good night, Karen," said Hannie and Nancy.

"Night," I mumbled.

I hurried into the tent I was sharing with

Becky. We said good night, then I crawled into my sleeping bag. But I could not fall asleep.

I heard noises in the woods. *Hoo. Hoo. Crick, crick. Whoosh!* They grew louder and louder. *HOO. HOO. CRICK, CRICK. WHOOSH!*

I jumped out of my sleeping bag and ran to Nora's tent. I was crying. "Nora, Nora, wake up! I am scared!" I said.

Nora put her arms around me. I told her all the things that were scaring me.

"You know, Karen, I was thinking that maybe this week you have been afraid, not bored. This is your first time at camp without Kristy, isn't it?" said Nora.

I nodded.

"Well, maybe it is scary without her and the other big kids who were here last time. Maybe you have been acting bored to cover up for being afraid," said Nora.

"Maybe. I am not really sure," I replied. "But I feel much better now anyway. Thank you."

94

I crawled into my own tent. This time I fell asleep. But I was very tired the next day.

We had an awards ceremony back at camp and I slept through the whole thing. I slept all the way home on the bus, too. I think the kids were singing "Big Blue Frog," and "B-I-N-G-O." But I am not sure.

When I woke up, someone was calling, "Karen! Karen, you're back!" It was Andrew.

I tumbled out of the bus and into the arms of my little-house and big-house families. I could tell they were happy to see me. And I sure was happy to see them.

Mail

I was glad to be home. My dolls wanted to know about camp. I told them everything.

Then I said, "Maybe I will go again next year. Only I think I will just try to have fun, and not be a know-it-all *or* a scaredy-cat."

They thought that was a good idea.

"Karen, here's some mail here for you," called Mommy.

Hurray! Mail. That is one of the best things about going to camp. When you come home you get lots of letters from your camp friends. I knew that Hannie, Nancy, David Michael, and Linny were writing and receiving letters, too.

Dear Karen,
   How are you? I hope you are not scared anymor. Next summer if you get scared, you can wake me up, okay?
   Are you going bak to Camp Mohawk? I asked my parents if I could go, and they said yes. I hope I wil see you there.

   Please writ back soon.
                          Love,
                             Becky

Hi, Nancy,
   It's me, Christine. How are you? How is your brother Danny? How is your cat Pokey? I bet they were happy to see you. My dog, Buffy, was very happy to see me.
   I am glad we became such good friends.
98

My mommy and daddy said that New Jersey is not too far from Stoneybrook. So we can visit each other. I hope you will come see me soon.

Love,
Christine

Dear Jill,
    I am definitely going back to camp next year. Can you believe it, next summer we will be eights. Then we will be nines, tens, elevens, twelves, thirteens! That means we will be CITs. I can hardly wait!
    Write soon.

Love,
Hannie

Hi, David Michael,
    How are you? Ach oo! Just kidding.
    I just want to tell you that you wer the best big brother I ever had. You wer also the only big brother I ever had. In reel life I have a baby sister.

Are you going back to camp next year?
Pleas say yes.

> Your litle brother,
> Wilson

Hi, Rick,
   Here is a neat stone I found in my back-
yard. I am still camping out while the
weather is warm.
   Thanks for a great summer.

> Linny (Nature Boy)

DEAR NORA,
   THANK YOU FOR BEING SUCH A GREAT COUN-
SELOR. WHEN I WAS NOT BEING A KNOW-it-ALL
OR A SCAREDY-CAT, I HAD A LOT OF FUN. IF I GO
BACK NEXT SUMMER, I WILL ONLY HAVE FUN —
NONE OF the OTHER STUFF.
   I WAS SO HAPPY TO SEE KRISTY. I THINK
MAYBE YOU WERE RIGHT. I REALLY DID MISS
HER A LOT.

100

AND NOW I MISS YOU. OH, WELL. I GUESS
YOU CAN ALWAYS MISS SOMEONE. SO
YOU MAY AS WELL HAVE FUN AND THEN YOU
WILL SEE THAT PERSON AGAIN BEFORE
YOU KNOW IT.

Love,
YOUR BRAVEST CAMPER, KAREN

Karen's Cool Campout Activities

You're Here Because You're Here!

Where are you? You're at the activity pages in the back of this Baby-sitters Little Sister Super Special! And you will be glad you're here, because there are all sorts of gigundoly fun camping things to make and do. So what are you waiting for? Turn the page. That's where the fun begins! (You can find the answers to the puzzles on pages 131–133 of this book.)

Bring on the Puzzles!

Is it a rainy day? Are you stuck in the bunk with nothing to do? Well, never fear. Karen's camping puzzles will keep you from becoming B-O-R-E-D!

Wild and Wacky Wordsearch

Linny and Wilson had a great time telling the story of the teeny tiny man. How many times can you find the words TEENY and TINY in this word-search? Don't forget to look up, down, sideways, backwards, and diagonally!

```
T E E N Y T
I N T N N E
N I I T E E
Y T N E E N
Y N E E T Y
T E Y N I T
T I N Y N I
T E E N Y N
E Y T Y N Y
E N N T E N
N I Y I E I
Y T I N T T
```

The Pumpkin Patch

There are eight pumpkins at the county fair. Can you find the two that are exactly alike?

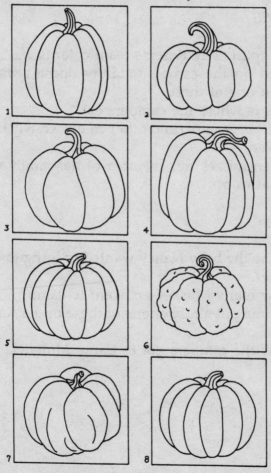

It's a Camping Crossword Puzzle!

Can you fill in the squares in this crossword puzzle? Use the clues to help you.

ACROSS

1. On sports day Karen's team color is _____.
3. Even on the campout, Linny doesn't want to sleep in one of these.
4. This is where the campers eat.
6. What bees, ants, and other creepy crawly things are called.
7. Karen misses this member of her family when she is at camp.

DOWN

2. Name the baby Nancy wanted to bring to camp with her.
3. How many Musketeers went to camp?
5. Hannie put a rubber one of these under Karen's backpack.
6. How the campers got to Camp Mohawk.

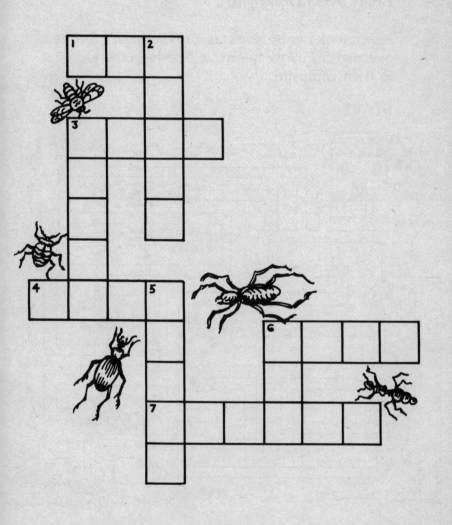

Going on an Overnight!

Karen took her bunkies far into the woods for their overnight. Follow the maze and help the girls get to their campsite.

START

FINISH

KRISTY THOMAS
1210 McLELLAND ROAD
STONEYBROOK, CONNECTICUT
06800

Letters Home

Karen and her pals write letters to their families at rest hour. How many words can you make with the letters in the words CAMP MOHAWK? Hannie has already done two for you!

MAP

HOP

_____   _____
_____   _____
_____   _____
_____   _____

You're Not Alone!

Linny is a nature boy. And nothing makes him happier than being with forest animals. There are two raccoons, three bluebirds, one squirrel, four bats, and a bear cub hidden in this forest picture. Can you find them all?

Sing Along!

When you're on a hike, singing makes the walking even more fun! Here are some super songs you can sing with your friends. Hannie, Nancy, and Karen think they are gigundoly fun.

The Ants Go Marching

The ants go marching one by one,
hurrah, hurrah.
The ants go marching one by one,
hurrah, hurrah.
The ants go marching one by one,
the little one stops to suck his thumb
and they all go marching down into the ground
to get out of the rain.
Boom boom boom.
The ants go marching two by two,
hurrah, hurrah.
The ants go marching two by two,
hurrah, hurrah.
The ants go marching two by two,
the little one stops to tie his shoe
and they all go marching down into the ground
to get out of the rain.
Boom boom boom.
(Now keep going using these words.)

Three . . . touch his knee.
Four . . . shut the door.
Five . . . see the hive.
Six . . . pick up sticks.
Seven . . . go to heaven.
Eight . . . open the gate.
Nine . . . sit on his behind.
Ten . . . to start again.

Ooey Gooey!

(Gross-out alert! This song is really yucky!)

Camp food's made of ooey gooey gopher guts
mutilated monkey meat
little birdies' dirty feet.
All wrapped up in all-purpose porpoise puss
and I forgot my spoon!
Oh no!

One Hundred Bottles of Pop

One hundred bottles of pop on the wall
One hundred bottles of pop
You take one down and pass it around
Ninety-nine bottles of pop on the wall!

Ninety-nine bottles of pop on the wall
Ninety-nine bottles of pop
You take one down and pass it around
Ninety-eight bottles of pop on the wall!

Now keep counting backward until you reach zero
bottles of pop on the wall.

Arts and Crafts Time!

Nancy and Christine like to go to arts and crafts. Here are some of the great things they have made.

Acorn Dolls

You will need:

1 acorn
2 small stones
a paintbrush
blue, black, and red tempera paint
six strands of yarn
two strands of a different color yarn
modeling clay
clear nail polish
glue

Here's what you do:

1. Paint a face on your acorn.
2. Make two braids using three pieces of yarn for each braid. Then tie the strands of different-colored yarn in bows on the ends of the braids.
3. Glue the braids to the sides of your acorn face.
4. Use the modeling clay to make your doll's body.
5. Set the acorn head on the body. Glue it into place.

6. Use the small stones as feet. Glue them to the bottom of your clay body.

7. Let the modeling clay dry for two days.

8. Paint the modeling clay.

9. When the paint dries, coat your whole doll with clear nail polish. Allow the polish to dry before you play with your doll.

Tie-Dye T-Shirts

This is mega-messy! Wear your oldest clothes, because anything the dye touches will be permanently dyed. *Be sure to make your tie-dye shirt with the help of an adult.*

You will need:

1 white T-shirt
one, two, or three colors of clothing dyes (depending on how colorful you want your shirt to be)
rubber bands
a pail
rubber or latex gloves

Here's what you do:

1. Gather up a section of the T-shirt and tie it tightly with a rubber band, as you see in the picture.

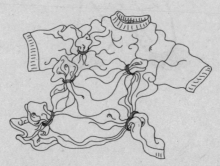

2. Twist a second rubber band halfway down from the first.

3. Repeat step two in other places on your shirt, as you see in the picture. You can gather as many sections as you want.

4. Pour the lightest color dye into the pail. Follow the directions on the box to mix the dye with the right amount of water. Ask an adult to handle the hot water part and to mix the dye.

5. Put on your gloves. (Do not touch the dye with your bare hands!) Dip the shirt completely into the dye. When it is covered in dye, remove the shirt from the pail and ring it out.

6. Clean out the pail. (*Be sure to dump the dye only into a stainless steel sink or tub. It will stain ceramic tile!*) If you are using only one color, skip to step nine. Otherwise, pour in a new, slightly darker color. Follow the directions to mix the dye with water. Again, you will need an adult to help with this part.

7. Now dip each of the gathered sections of your shirt into the pail. The darker dye will cover the lighter color, so don't dip the gathers all the way — leave some of the first color showing on your shirt.

8. Now repeat steps six and seven, using the darkest color. Dip only the very ends of the gathered sections into this color. Leave the other sections as they are.

9. Let the T-shirt dry without removing the rubber bands. When the shirt is completely dry, remove the rubber bands and rinse your shirt in cold water. Be sure to wash the shirt by itself a few times before putting it in with other clothes.

Daisy Chains

You will need:

pencil
scissors
paste or glue
white, green, and yellow construction paper
oak tag or poster board

Here's what you do:

1. Draw a daisy (see picture), a medium-sized circle, and a leaf on your oak tag.

2. Cut the drawings from the oak tag. These are your stencils.

3. Trace 30 daisies onto the white paper. Cut them out.

4. Now trace 30 circles onto the yellow paper. Cut them out.

5. Trace 15 leaves onto the green paper. Cut them out.

6. Glue one yellow circle to the center of each daisy.

7. Glue the flowers together as you see in the picture. They will form a circle you can fit over your head.

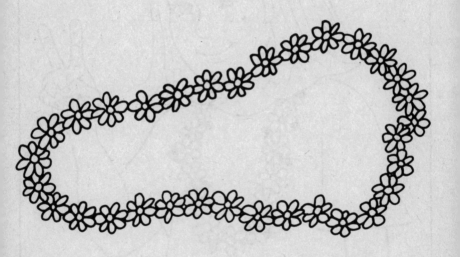

8. Glue the green leaves to the bottom of *some* of your flowers. (If you want more leaves, repeat step 5.)

Now wear your pretty necklace. Talk about flower power!

Leapin' Lanyards!

Every but *every* camper makes lanyards — necklaces made of long plastic strings. Kids wear them around their neck and dangle whistles or keychains from them. The most popular lanyard stitch is the box stitch. The box stitch may seem tough to do, but before you get boxed in, read these simple instructions.

You will need:

two different colored strands of lanyard, each six feet long
one lanyard hook

Here's what you do:

1. Thread the strings through the lanyard hook so that three feet of each lanyard hangs on either side of the hook.
2. Let's say that your lanyard is pink and black. Loop one side of the black lanyard toward you. Loop the other side away from you. Look at the picture to see what your loops should look like.
3. Now take the side of the pink lanyard that is closest to you. Thread that side over the near black loop and under the far one.
4. Take the side of the pink lanyard that is furthest from you and thread it over the far black loop and under the near black loop. Pull all four strands tightly. That is one stitch.
5. Now loop one pink strand of lanyard toward you. Loop the other pink strand away from you. The pink strands will look just like the black strands in the picture next to step number two.
6. Take the strand of black lanyard that is closest to you and thread it over the the near pink loop and under the far one.

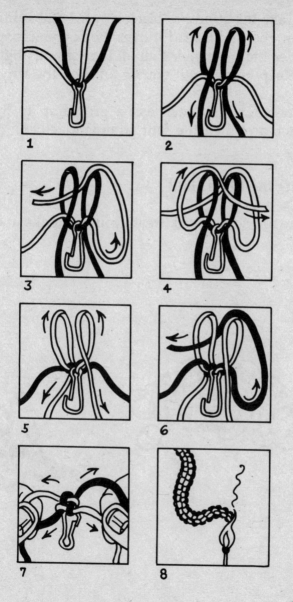

7. Take the strand of black lanyard that is furthest from you and thread it over the far pink loop and under the near one. Pull all four strands tightly.
8. Keep going until you've finished the lanyard.

After your last stitch ask a grown-up to light a match and melt the four strands together.

Enter the Mess Hall!

Here are some quick treats you can make and eat!

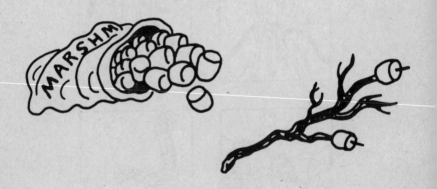

No-Cook Hot Dogs

You will need:

three slices of thinly sliced bologna
2 slices of swiss cheese
1 hot dog roll
mustard
relish

Here's what you do:

Layer your food this way — bologna, swiss cheese, bologna, swiss cheese, bologna. Roll your food up tightly until it looks like a thick hot dog. Put your dog in the roll. Top with mustard and relish and take a bite!

Marshmallow Taffy

You will need:

two marshmallows

Here's what you do:

Use your fingers to squish the two marshmallows together. Now tug and pull at the marshmallows until they are turned inside out, and the sugary outside is mixed in with the gooey inside. Keep going until the marshmallow takes on a hard, taffy-like feel. Now eat your taffy or use it to make . . .

No-Cook S'mores

If you can't get to a campfire, these tasty treats are the next best thing!

You will need:

marshmallow taffy
graham crackers
one chocolate bar

Here's what you do:

Leave your chocolate bar in a sunny place until it becomes warm. Place a piece of warmed chocolate and some marshmallow taffy on a graham cracker. Top them with a second graham cracker. Now, take a bite! YUMMY!

127

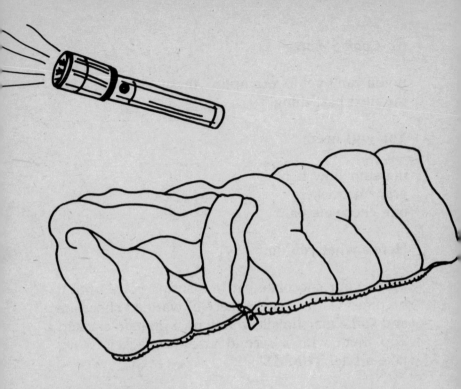

Summer Reading

Rest hour usually comes right after lunch. It's a great time to lie around the bunk and read or write letters. Here are some fun camp books to read:

The Bobbsey Twins Go Camping by Laura L. Hope
Bummer Summer by Ann M. Martin
Color War! by Marilyn Kaye
The Cut-Ups at Camp Custer by James Marshall

Campout Ha-Has!

What do you do when you hear *ha ha ha ha*?
Find out where the jokes are coming from!

Search no further. The funniest camp jokes around
are right here. Karen thinks they are gigundoly
funny!

How do you keep a skunk under the bunk from
smelling?
Hold its nose!

What do you get when you mix a Tyrannosaurus Rox with a skunk?
The biggest stinker in the world!

Is it okay to eat the sand at the beach?
Why eat sand when you can eat dirt cheap?

What shampoo works best on mountains?
Head and Boulders!

What's the best way to catch a fish?
Have someone throw it to you!

Why is softball a monster camper's favorite sport?
Because of all the double headers!

Answers to the Puzzle Pages

Wild and Wacky Wordsearch

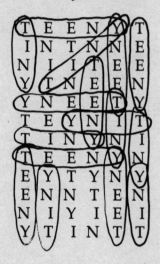

The Pumpkin Patch

It's a Camping Crossword Puzzle

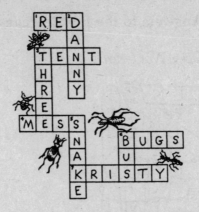

Going on an Overnight!

START

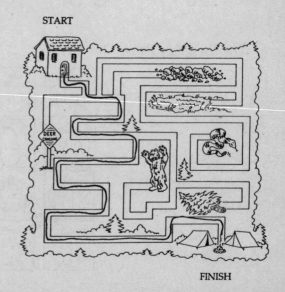

FINISH

Letters Home

Here are ten words. How many others did you find?
MAP, HOP, HAWK, HAM, CAP, WHAM, MOP, PACK, HACK, MOW

You're Not Alone!

About the Author

ANN M. MARTIN lives in New York City and loves animals, especially cats. She has two cats of her own, Mouse and Rosie.

Other books by Ann M. Martin that you might enjoy are *Stage Fright*; *Me and Katie (the Pest)*; and the books in *The Baby-sitters Club* series.

Ann likes ice cream and *I Love Lucy*. And she has her own little sister, whose name is Jane.

LITTLE APPLE®

BABY·SITTERS
Little Sister™
by Ann M. Martin, author of *The Baby-sitters Club*®

☐ MQ44300-3	#1	Karen's Witch	$2.75
☐ MQ44259-7	#2	Karen's Roller Skates	$2.75
☐ MQ44299-7	#3	Karen's Worst Day	$2.75
☐ MQ44264-3	#4	Karen's Kittycat Club	$2.75
☐ MQ44258-9	#5	Karen's School Picture	$2.75
☐ MQ44298-8	#6	Karen's Little Sister	$2.75
☐ MQ44257-0	#7	Karen's Birthday	$2.75
☐ MQ42670-2	#8	Karen's Haircut	$2.75
☐ MQ43652-X	#9	Karen's Sleepover	$2.75
☐ MQ43651-1	#10	Karen's Grandmothers	$2.75
☐ MQ43650-3	#11	Karen's Prize	$2.75
☐ MQ43649-X	#12	Karen's Ghost	$2.95
☐ MQ43648-1	#13	Karen's Surprise	$2.75
☐ MQ43646-5	#14	Karen's New Year	$2.75
☐ MQ43645-7	#15	Karen's in Love	$2.75
☐ MQ43644-9	#16	Karen's Goldfish	$2.75
☐ MQ43643-0	#17	Karen's Brothers	$2.75
☐ MQ43642-2	#18	Karen's Home-Run	$2.75
☐ MQ43641-4	#19	Karen's Good-Bye	$2.95
☐ MQ44823-4	#20	Karen's Carnival	$2.75
☐ MQ44824-2	#21	Karen's New Teacher	$2.95
☐ MQ44833-1	#22	Karen's Little Witch	$2.95
☐ MQ44832-3	#23	Karen's Doll	$2.95

More Titles... ➡

Enter Karen's

BABY·SITTERS

Little Sister®

Summer Friendship Giveaway!

Karen would never go to camp without her super special stationery kit — and now you can win a kit of your very own! Just fill in the coupon below and return it by October 31, 1993. Each of the **500 winners** will receive a **Baby-sitters Little Sister Stationery Kit** filled with postcards, stickers, a pad, and a sparkle pen!

500 WINNERS!

Fill in the coupon below or write the information on a 3" x 5" piece of paper and mail to:

BABY-SITTERS LITTLE SISTER SUMMER FRIENDSHIP GIVEAWAY, P.O. Box 7500, Jefferson City, MO 65102.

Canadian residents send entries to: Iris Ferguson, Scholastic Inc., 123 Newkirk Road, Richmond Hill, Ontario, Canada L4C 3G5.

- -

Name_____ Date of Birth _____

Street _____

City _____ State/Zip _____

Where did you buy this Baby-sitters Little Sister book?

❑ Bookstore   ❑ Drugstore   ❑ Supermarket   ❑ Library

❑ Book Club   ❑ Book Fair   ❑ Other_____(specify)

BLS793

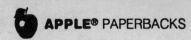